## The Ghost on the Roof

THE BLACKSMITH came fully awake, and his gaze shot upward at the roof of the coach.

"Merciful powers!" he said, and laughed. "He's come for a ride! It's The Great Chaffalo! With his watch as big as a turnip!"

"Chaffalo?" Touch muttered.

"The magician! The haunt, lad! If you want to see a live ghost, stick your head out the window. He's on the roof."

Touch wasn't certain that he wanted to lay eyes on a haunt, but he stuck his head out into the rain.

In the pale light of the coach lantern, he could see the coachman with his face turned back. And on the roof, he caught sight of a long leather boot glistening in the rain.

# ALSO BY
# SID FLEISCHMAN

# THE
# MIDNIGHT
# HORSE

# SID FLEISCHMAN

# THE
# MIDNIGHT
# HORSE

## ILLUSTRATIONS BY PETER SÍS

A Greenwillow Book

HarperTrophy®
*An Imprint of HarperCollinsPublishers*

*For Seth and Dana*

Harper Trophy® is a registered trademark
of HarperCollins Publishers Inc.

The Midnight Horse
Text copyright © 1990 by Sid Fleischman, Inc.
Illustrations copyright © 1990 by Peter Sís

Library of Congress Cataloging-in-Publication Data
Fleischman, Sid.
The midnight horse / Sid Fleischman.
p. cm.
"Greenwillow Books."
Summary: Touch enlists the help of The Great Chaffalo, a ghostly magician,
to thwart his great-uncle's plans to put Touch into the orphan house and
swindle The Red Raven Inn away from Miss Sally.
ISBN 0-688-09441-4 — ISBN 0-06-072216-9 (pbk.)
[1. Adventure and adventurers—Fiction. 2. Magicians—Fiction. 3. Ghosts—
Fiction. 4. Orphans—Fiction.] I. Title.
PZ7.F5992Mk 1990                                      89-23441
[Fic]—dc20                                                CIP
                                                          AC

First Harper Trophy edition, 2004
11  12  13  14   CG/CW   10  9  8

Visit us on the World Wide Web!
www.harperchildrens.com

# CONTENTS

# CONTENTS

# THE
# MIDNIGHT
# HORSE

# CHAPTER
## I

# *The Man on the Roof*

It was raining bullfrogs. The coach lurched and swayed along the river road like a ship in rough seas. Inside clung three passengers like unlashed cargo.

One was a blacksmith, another was a thief, and the third was an orphan boy named Touch.

Touch was skinny and bareheaded, with hair as curly as wood shavings. Despite the blustering April night, he felt in the best of spirits. He'd never ridden high and mighty in a coach before, and meant to enjoy every passing mile. His usual way of travel was on his two lanky legs.

"Raining bullfrogs," the blacksmith said again.

"I noticed," said Touch.

"Boy, is that your stomach growling? You hungry, lad? You're so thin a body would have to shake out your clothes to find you. Touch is your name, is it?"

Touch's clothes were, in fact, acres too big, but they were the best fit he'd been able to get from a ragman's castoffs in Portsmouth. In the lining of the coat he'd found a gold piece hidden away, and that had enabled him to give up the fine art of walking, for the coach.

The blacksmith dug into one of his pockets and produced a lump of dark bread. "Put this in your stomach, lad."

Touch accepted the bread with thanks, but added, "A crumb or two will suit me. I expect my great-uncle will have a feast laid out for me when we get to Cricklewood. We never met before, but I wrote him a letter I was coming."

"Who's your great-uncle?"

"Wigglesforth. Judge Henry Wigglesforth. Maybe you know him."

The blacksmith's hand, big enough to span a pie plate, gave his jaws a scratching, thoughtful rub. "Of course I do, Touch. Everybody does."

A blast of thunder filled the air, and the thief took a quick look back over his shoulder. He was a long-armed man with his face wrapped around with a great brown muffler so that he looked to Touch like a loosely wrapped mummy. Glancing back over his shoulder seemed to be habit, for Touch had noticed him do it before, as if the man thought someone might be following him.

"Stranger, what did you say your name was?" asked the blacksmith.

"I didn't," answered the thief. In fact, he had, but he changed his name more often than his stockings, and now he couldn't remember what name he'd bestowed upon himself.

"I thought you said Cratt."

"Otis Cratt," added Touch, as if to confirm the blacksmith's memory.

A short grumble shot through the mummy wrappings. "Then that must be my name. Otis Cratt, to be sure. And good-night."

He locked his arms as if to sleep. But hours later

when the blacksmith checked through his leather billfold, Touch noticed Otis Cratt's eyes drawn to it like a compass needle to true north.

After a while, Mr. Hobbs, for that was the blacksmith's name, fell into a contented doze. Touch was content to watch the rain.

In a flash of lightning, he caught sight of Otis Cratt's long arm. It was weaving like a snake stalking its prey, reaching out for the blacksmith's billfold.

Touch was too astonished to speak.

The chiming of a watch lifted the blacksmith's eyelids. The thieving hand retreated in a flash. Mr. Hobbs hauled up the gold chain across his vest to glance at his watch. But there was no watch at the end of the chain.

Sleepily, the blacksmith chuckled and poked the empty end of the chain back into his vest pocket. Otis Cratt rewrapped the muffler around his face. But not before Touch had got a look. A face rough as moldy cheese, and eyes as deep as knotholes.

But a watch continued striking the hour overhead, as clear as church bells.

The blacksmith came fully awake, and his gaze

4

shot upward at the roof of the coach. "Merciful powers!" he said, and laughed. "He's come for a ride! It's The Great Chaffalo! With his watch as big as a turnip!"

"Chaffalo?" Touch muttered.

"The magician! The haunt, lad! If you want to see a live ghost, stick your head out the window. He's on the roof."

Touch wasn't certain that he wanted to lay eyes on a haunt, but he stuck his head out into the rain.

In the pale light of the coach lantern, he could see the coachman with his face turned back. And on the roof, he caught sight of a long leather boot glistening in the rain.

A merry voice shot through the air. "Drive on, coachman! And watch that pothole dead ahead!"

Touch was surprised that his heart wasn't in his throat. He blinked away the rain and wished he could see better.

They hit the pothole, and Mr. Hobbs grabbed Touch by the collar to keep him from flying out the window.

"Did you get a good look?" asked the blacksmith, hauling Touch back into the coach. "He ain't shy,

that one. He was famous once. That chiming watch was given him by the King of Prussia."

Otis Cratt sat unconcerned, wrapped in his muffler against the cold.

Touch wondered if Chaffalo might come swinging through a window for the shelter of the coach. But he didn't, and when another hour passed without the chiming of a watch, Mr. Hobbs said that he was gone.

At last, the skies gave a last snort of thunder and a final sneeze of rain.

And at last, the coachman snuffed out his side lanterns. Dawn was rising as bright as a marigold when the village came into view.

Through the window Touch saw a sign nailed to a tree.

**Cricklewood**
NEW HAMPSHIRE

---

**Population 217**
**216 Fine Folks**
**&**
**1 Infernal Grouch**

Touch read it aloud and then asked, "Who's the grouch?"

The blacksmith gave his chin a rub. "I hate to tell you this, Touch. But it's your great-uncle Wigglesforth."

# CHAPTER
# 2

# *The Great Chaffalo*

THE COACH pulled into The Red Raven Inn, and the passengers alighted. Touch gazed at the roof, as if The Great Chaffalo might still be hanging on. The thief, with a backward look, strode off into the trees.

"He meant to snatch your wallet," Touch said to Mr. Hobbs.

"And leap from the coach?" remarked the blacksmith, mildly surprised. "The man must be a fool. But he'll bear watching."

Touch followed Mr. Hobbs through the inn door.

"Lad, don't be too disappointed if your great-uncle forgot you're coming," said the blacksmith. "You know how it is with a judge, his head all spiderwebbed with laws and contracts. Bound to make a man forgetful."

They entered the public room, where a meager fire was doing its best to blaze up a welcome.

Touch saw pictures hanging about the walls, but not a living soul hanging about the room. His heart dropped, but only a little. Disappointments were as common as pig tracks, in his experience, and he shrugged off this one with no more effort than a tree sheds a leaf.

"Reckon I'll have a look around the village, now that I'm here," he said. His great-uncle was, after all, merely another stranger in his life. Only the found gold piece had put him in mind. Still, Touch was curious to have a look at his only living relative. If the man was a grouch, so much the better, and Touch would be on his way again.

The blacksmith gave a shout. "Sally, where are you? We could use a hearty breakfast."

"Not me, sir," said Touch. "I've hardly a copper penny left to spend."

A girl of seventeen or eighteen came rushing

down the stairs. She had a pretty face with a sorrow-struck look in her eyes. Touch thought she must have been upstairs, crying them out. But now they brightened, like sudden blue sky, when she saw the blacksmith.

"Mr. Hobbs! I didn't hear the coach."

"You weren't listening. I think you've lost the habit, Sally."

"I missed you! I trust your business went well."

"Splendid! Splendid!" declared the blacksmith, but Touch detected a certain pretense in his cheeriness.

"I'll build up the fire," said Sally. "Winter's hanging on like a bad cold, isn't it? And here it is, almost May."

"We'll tend to the fire. Touch, you have the pleasure of meeting our innkeeper, Miss Sally Hoskins. Breakfast for two, Sally. And this is Touch, with hardly a copper penny in his pocket. You wouldn't turn away a hungry boy, would you?"

She gave a little smile and hurried off to the kitchen. The blacksmith's eyes followed her. They turned suddenly as sad as her own.

"Isn't there anyone staying at the inn?" Touch asked.

"Hardly a soul anymore, lad."

"Is it haunted?"

"You might say, and you might not." The blacksmith seemed to reach urgently for a new subject of conversation and pointed to a framed picture on the wall. "Touch, look there! At that poster. It's The Great Chaffalo in his prime. And autographed in his own hand!"

Touch crossed to the theatrical poster. In a blaze of colors, it showed a tall, smiling man in evening dress with a red sash across his chest. His outstretched fingers were shooting lightning bolts toward a yellow horse in a cloud of straw. Large green letters proclaimed:

---

**THE WONDER SHOW!**

**SEE THE GREAT CHAFFALO
PERFORM
HIS WORLD-FAMOUS
HORSE TRICK!**

---

"He was born right here in Cricklewood," said the blacksmith. "And he built himself a summer house, where he would rest after his travels. He'd sometimes take his meals here at The Red Raven. I was just a boy then, and he once pinched a Chinese coin off the tip of my nose!"

Touch stared into the magician's eyes, and they appeared to gaze back. "What was the world-famous horse trick?"

"He'd snap his fingers and turn a pile of straw into a prancing horse."

"I declare!" said Touch.

"The Great Chaffalo became a ghost by mistake, you might say," remarked the blacksmith. "He was doing his horse trick on a Mississippi showboat. According to the papers, a mule skinner stood up and shouted, 'Chaffalo, if you're so great, let's see you catch this bullet in your teeth!' And Chaffalo might have, too, but the mule skinner's aim was way off the mark. The lead ball knocked The Great Chaffalo into an early grave."

"How did his ghost get all the way back here?" Touch asked, unable to take his eyes off the wonders of the poster.

"Walked," answered the blacksmith. "Walked or rode the coaches. And got all tangled up in the Civil War. At the Battle of Pea Ridge, a wounded soldier claimed a fellow had come along and changed a bundle of straw into a horse for him to ride. It was in the newspapers. Same thing at Shiloh and Yorktown. And I suppose when The Great Chaffalo got tired of walking and riding coach roofs, he just made himself a horse. And rode home to Cricklewood, happy as a lark."

"Is that house he built close by?"

"Out in the woods, and kind of fallen in. Hardly anyone goes out there anymore, the place being truly haunted."

"But he sounds such a friendly spirit," Touch remarked.

"Haunts are haunts," said the blacksmith.

Mr. Hobbs returned to the fireplace, where Sally had come and gone, leaving two steaming mugs of coffee.

"Drink up and warm up, Touch," said the blacksmith. "And tell me what you aim to make of yourself."

"I reckoned on going to sea," Touch replied.

"To sea! Don't tell me!"

Touch warmed his hands around the coffee mug. "I signed on as cabin boy, but the ship went aground before we cleared the harbor. The captain figured me for a Jonah. That's bad luck on two feet, sir."

"Was it wagging tongues that nipped your seagoing career in the bud?" asked the blacksmith.

"Quick as lightning," Touch replied. "I couldn't show my face along the wharves after that without stones thrown at me."

"Young Touch," Mr. Hobbs said softly. "You don't believe you're bad luck on two legs, do you?"

Touch hesitated. "I don't know, sir. Sometimes I reckon I am."

It surprised Touch to find himself so easily revealing his grievous secret to the blacksmith. He'd hoped to leave his Jonahed self behind in Portsmouth.

Mr. Hobbs peered at Touch. "If folks called you a dog, would you start barking and scratching for fleas?"

"No, sir," Touch muttered.

"Folks talk rubbish!" The blacksmith leaned forward and lowered his voice. "Touch, it was rubbish that's brought Sally so low, as you're bound to find out. Wagging tongues!"

Touch glanced around at the heavy emptiness of the public room. "Kind of haunted and kind of not, you said."

"Worse."

"By dogs!" said Touch, wondering what could be worse.

"A barber with gold teeth signed the register last October to stay the night. Gold teeth, uppers and lowers, Touch. He was never seen again. Disappeared."

"Skipped without paying his bill?"

"Not likely. His barber's box was left behind. And someone got to wagging his tongue that maybe Sally's own pa murdered him. For the gold teeth, you see. Crime and motive, neat as a pin. There's still village mutterings of spading up the grounds for the bones. Sally's pa worried himself into a grave of his own. But the tongues still wag, and travelers avoid The Red Raven."

"Was Sally crying?"

"She hardly stops," replied the blacksmith. "And

I wouldn't mention you're Judge Wigglesforth's great-nephew."

"It was him, then," said Touch.

"It was him started the gossip."

# CHAPTER
# 3
# *Thirty-*
# *seven*
# *Cents*

As far as Touch could tell, Judge Wigglesforth had the grandest house in the village. It stood amid a thick stand of birch trees on a steep hillside. A long flight of plank stairs tumbled down from the front door like a tongue hanging out.

As Touch climbed the planks, it seemed to him that every window was peeping at him. Hesitating for only a moment, he reached up for the brass door knocker and banged away. And banged away again.

It seemed an eternity before the door swung open.

There stood a large man with eyes as wet and baggy as live oysters. He was dressed in black and wore a choke-me-to-death starched collar.

"Morning, Uncle. I'm Touch."

"Wipe the mud off your shoes," Judge Wigglesforth said in a quick, scornful voice. "You see the scraper, don't you? It's not against the law to use it. This isn't a stable."

"Yes, Uncle."

"You won't call me Uncle. I'm Judge to you like everybody else."

"Yes, Judge."

Touch scraped the mud off his shoes and then followed the judge into the entry. Almost at once Touch saw a long brown muffler hanging from a clothes tree near the door. He'd seen it before, and his mind began to spin. Had Otis Cratt made straight here from the coach?

"If you've got a caller," said Touch, "I'll come back another time."

"I've got no callers," replied Judge Wigglesforth. "Do you steal?"

"What, sir?"

"I never saw a boy who didn't steal. And no doubt you curse."

Touch felt his back stiffen. His great-uncle meant to bully him. "I've been known to curse," he answered firmly.

"Be warned. I'll fine you five cents a word for swearing. I go by the law books, chapter and verse!"

"Yes, sir."

"Let's not waste time. I expect you came seeking your inheritance."

Touch was caught by enormous surprise. An inheritance? He didn't know that he had one. But in as even a voice as he could manage, he said, "You seen clear through me, Judge. That's what I came for."

The judge cracked a thin smile. "You're a shifty-eyed boy."

"I didn't know that, sir," Touch replied coolly.

"Did your pa tell you I offered to bring him up in the law? In my own footsteps!"

"No, sir."

"But the ungrateful fool ran off to sea, leaving his affairs in my hands. And now here's his whelp on my doorstep." The judge was breathing like a bellows. "Don't expect me to take pity and put a roof over your orphan head. And feed you until you're grown."

"No, sir," replied Touch, with immense relief.

"I won't have a brat underfoot."

"Can't blame you," said Touch. "Boys are terrible pesky to have around. Now you've found me out, being shifty and all, I'll pick up whatever Pa left me and be on my way."

"Your inheritance is spent."

"Not by me, it wasn't," said Touch quickly.

"Don't get cheeky with me," snapped the judge. "I'll have you arrested for breaking the law."

"What law?"

"Whistling on the Sabbath."

"You've got the days of the week mixed up, Judge. It ain't Sunday. And the only thing whistling is the wind. You might as well arrest God Himself."

The old man squared his shoulders. "You put your foot in the law now! Blaspheming Our Lord!"

Touch saw that he'd fallen into a trap. The judge had a mind crisscrossed with spiderwebs, as the blacksmith had said.

"In a court of law, I'd fine you two dollars," said the judge. "But I'll suspend the judgment on your solemn promise to say your prayers dutifully and watch your tongue."

Touch gave the smallest possible nod, and his great-uncle went rummaging through papers laid out on a desk. For the first time, Touch gazed about at the room. He'd seen junkyards with less plunder. There were great stacks of yellowing old newspapers, and boxes and barrels heaped with chipped crockery, pewter candlesticks, umbrellas, and old dusty top hats. Touch couldn't guess what else was tucked away. It was clear that the judge never threw anything out.

Once again, Touch's eyes fell on the brown muffler hanging in the hall, and the feeling came over him stronger than before that Otis Cratt was waiting out of sight. What business would Judge Wigglesforth have with a pickpocket of a man?

Touch wondered if he should reveal what he had seen in the coach. But he'd given a solemn promise to hold his tongue, and it suited him to hold it now.

"Sign here," called out his great-uncle, dipping a pen in ink.

Touch approached a document now spread open on the desk.

"What is it, sir?"

"A full and careful accounting of your pa's worldly

goods. Burial expenses, debts paid off, and legal expenses."

"But my pa was lost at sea. That don't cost a penny!"

"So he was. But don't try to instruct me in the law of *corpus delicti* and the rules of *malitia praecogitata*. Sign as you're told."

He's talking hogwash, Touch thought. He's making up new laws as he goes along, and trying to befuddle me with words you couldn't bust on an anvil.

"Sign, and let's be done with it," said Judge Wigglesforth, impatiently holding out the pen. "I've pressing business to attend to. This is merely a receipt to tidy up our affairs, boy, legal and proper. It says that you have accepted your full inheritance and will press no further claims upon me."

"Inheritance? You said it was spent."

"There's a small cash balance in your favor. And your pa's silver watch."

"His watch!" Touch felt a yearning rush to own something of his pa's. "I'd hugely love to see it, sir."

The judge went poking around among his boxes. He finally hauled up a chain with a silver watch dangling on the end like an unlucky fish.

The watch had stopped ticking years ago. But Touch closed a hand around it, and his heart began to beat away. He felt for an awesome moment that he was holding his pa's own hand in his. He found himself close to a rise of tears.

But as he opened his fingers to wind the watch, his eyes caught the initials engraved on the back. They weren't his pa's initials. This had never been his pa's watch.

"Take the pen, boy, and sign for it. And here's the cash money left over and due you."

Touch stared at his great-uncle. Judge Wigglesforth began to pinch out coins on the table. He counted them aloud, one by one, as if it pained him to part with a single copper.

"It totals to thirty-seven cents. That's a powerful sum for a boy your age to come into."

Anger was blazing up inside Touch. His great-uncle was not only a cunning rascal, but a miser. "Keep the confounded thirty-seven cents, same as everything else my pa left. And I won't need this watch. I never had much need for the time of day."

The judge glared. "Sign for what's yours!"

"No, sir."

"What?"

"I don't choose to put my name to anything."

"Don't cross me, Nephew," warned the judge. "Put your name to this document, or I'll scratch out another! I'll commit you to the orphan house!"

"You'll have to catch me first," said Touch, and streaked for the door.

# On
# the Run

Touch avoided the flight of stairs and darted through the birch trees instead. And then, when he stopped to catch his breath, he stopped to think. What was he in a whirlwind hurry for? His great-uncle didn't have the legs to catch him.

To satisfy himself that the judge wasn't following, Touch climbed a tree to look back at the house. He sat for a while watching. He felt powerfully safe high up in the wet branches, where no one would think to look. He wished he could hide forever and let the world below go hang.

The world below suddenly caught Touch's eye again. From the rear of his great-uncle's house, he saw a man emerge. A man with his face wrapped with a muffler against the morning cold. A brown muffler.

Otis Cratt loped off into the deep woods like a wolf returning to its den. He stopped once to turn and look back at the house. Then he dipped a hand into his overcoat pocket and hauled up a small leather pouch.

He opened the drawstring and emptied the pouch into his hand. Three or four white beads tumbled out, as clearly as Touch could make them out. Light-fingered from the house, no doubt, he thought.

Or had his great-uncle given the pouch away? Well, it was no affair of his. He had other worries to worry. He didn't like the sound of that orphan house. He'd run off from one before, after his ma was struck down by winter fever. He chose to bring himself up, free as a sail to catch any chance wind that came along.

Otis Cratt was long out of sight when Touch climbed down and decided to head for The Red Raven Inn. He kept to the trees, to avoid being seen,

then slipped past Sally's barn and stables. He let himself in through the kitchen door and gave a quiet call.

"Sally. Miss Sally. It's me, Touch."

After a moment, she appeared at the head of the stairs with a shawl wrapped tightly around her. She seemed to brighten at the sight of a visitor, the way a morning glory opens to sunlight. "Come in and warm yourself," she said.

"I can sharpen your knives," he said in a rush. "I can chop stove wood, clean the chimneys, hammer a nail straight, and do a great heap of things."

She gave a little laugh. "What are you rattling on about? I can do those things for myself."

"I don't have any money and I need a safe place to be. Only until Judge Wigglesforth gives me up for gone. He'll never think to come looking for me livin' like a guest upstairs."

"Judge Wigglesforth."

Her smile faded away at the mention of his name, and Touch took a long, deep breath. "Truth is, he's my great-uncle."

Touch saw Sally's gaze sharpen, and he felt as welcome as weeds.

"It doesn't please me none, either," Touch said. "I'd sooner be first cousin to a stepped-on snake. But there it is. He's fiddled up some paper he wanted me to sign, but I wouldn't, and now he's madder'n lightning."

Sally gave a weary shrug. "He's a fine hand at fiddling up papers. He's left one here for me. The judge means to get The Red Raven for himself. He's offering hardly enough to pay for the candlesticks."

"Don't surprise me," said Touch. "My great-uncle is tighter'n a wet shirt."

Sally's voice fell away to little more than a whisper. "Mr. Hobbs is strongly against my signing the bill of sale. But debts are piling up, and there's the horrible talk about—"

She stopped herself.

"I know about the talk," Touch murmured. "The murdered man."

"Gossip! No one was murdered here."

"Yes, miss."

"The man disappeared like steam from a kettle. Like he was the devil himself."

"It don't scare me none," said Touch. "I'd be pleased to stay under your roof, if you'll allow me.

My great-uncle aims to cart me off to an orphan house, but not if he can't nab me."

"That horrid orphan house in Fallwater? It's not fit for mice!"

"I figure the judge is bound to give me up for lost after a few days, and I can slip away."

"I'll get Mr. Hobbs. He'll know what to do." And then Sally averted her eyes. "Touch, this is the last place you'll be safe. By nightfall, The Red Raven will belong to your great-uncle. Not half an hour ago I decided to sign his fiddling papers."

# A Place
# to Hide

Touch poked up the fire and waited. When he heard sounds in the courtyard, he knew it would be Sally returning with the blacksmith. But when he looked through the window, he saw Judge Wigglesforth driving up in a black buggy.

Touch quickly retreated up the stairs.

The bell jingled over the door as it opened, and Touch could hear footsteps across the creaking hardwood floor.

"Innkeeper! Where are you, girl!"

Touch's heart was booming like a bass drum in his ears. It seemed a wonder to him that his great-uncle couldn't hear it. But all fell silent down below. Touch felt emboldened to creep a step lower so that he could peep into the public room.

His great-uncle stood at the fireplace, warming his hands as if stealing all the heat he could, free of charge.

"That oaf!" the judge barked aloud into the fire-place, and Touch thought he must be growling about Touch himself. "That greedy, thickheaded jail-bird!"

No, it was Otis Cratt on his mind. And his mind, Touch thought, was considerably bristled.

"Turning up on my doorstep!" the judge rumbled on. "Another payment in advance, if you please! I shouldn't have written the bumbling fool to come back. He hasn't sense enough to hide himself away until I need him!"

The bell over the door rang out again, and the blacksmith strode in, followed by Sally, wrapped in her shawl. Mr. Hobbs, still in his leather apron, was

clearly surprised to find the judge instead of Touch standing by the fire.

"Good morning, Judge," said the blacksmith.

"That's a matter of opinion." The judge turned his oyster eyes at Sally. "There's a limit to my patience, Miss Hoskins. Have you signed the papers? The bill of sale?"

"No, she hasn't," declared the blacksmith.

"The girl can speak for herself," snapped Judge Wigglesforth.

The blacksmith glowered. "You're trying to buy The Red Raven for the price of a chicken coop."

"She won't get a better offer. This inn has a plague on it. I'm being charitable to offer anything at all!"

"When you talk charity, Judge, even the dogs and cats run for cover. Sally ain't ready to sell."

And in a thin voice, Sally added, "Perhaps I need a little more time to think it over."

"You've had weeks, girl. Make up your mind, yes or no. I've more important affairs to attend to. If I don't have your signature by tomorrow, you won't see me back. I'll withdraw my offer."

37

"That," said the blacksmith, "would be charitable. Good morning, Judge."

Touch watched his great-uncle pull in his neck and head for the door, his coattails flying. The bell left a merry jingle floating in the air, and the blacksmith burst into a laugh.

"But dear Mr. Hobbs," Sally said, "I can't let you keep trying to pay off The Red Raven's debts."

Touch remembered the blacksmith's empty watch chain. He wondered if Mr. Hobbs had left the village to sell his valuables, keeping it a secret from Sally.

"Trifling debts," said Mr. Hobbs, dismissing the matter with a wave of his hand. "This is where you were born and brought up. I don't intend to let the infernal rascal lay hands on it." And then he added, "Now you've signed, throw his papers into the fire."

"The inn will be better off closed and sold off," Sally murmured.

"And there's the mystification of it," said the blacksmith. "Why is the old skinflint so anxious to lay hands on a public inn with a plague on it, in his own words? Ah, Touch! There you are! What's this about you and your great-uncle?''

Touch explained about his unexpected inheritance, with all the howling expenses made against it.

"Thirty-seven cents left, mind you!" bellowed Mr. Hobbs. "Cheaper'n dirt, that man! Thirty-seven cents! You were right to sign nothing. If he was that anxious for your name on a document, there must be more of value left than meets the eye."

"It's the orphan house that worries me, sir," Touch declared.

"You can pick out a room and stay the night," Sally said brightly.

"But don't think your great-uncle will be so easy to run off from, now you've turned up," put in the blacksmith. "Is he your only live and breathing relative?"

"Yes, sir."

"Then I suppose he has the power to put you in the orphan house. He'll check every coach to see you haven't flown the village. Lad, he'll stick to you like a fishhook until he's swindled you legal out of what's coming to you."

Touch hesitated. "Would it go hard on Miss Sally

if he finds out I was tucked away here?"

"Harboring a runaway boy?" the blacksmith muttered. "If there ain't a law against it, your great-uncle will make one. You can depend upon it!"

# CHAPTER
# 6
# *A Bundle of Straw*

AFTER THE blacksmith left, Sally made a pot of tea and sat talking with Touch in her upstairs parlor. The sun was streaming in through the windows, yellow as butter, and they chattered away merrily as if to lift each other's gloom.

Touch told of his pa, who once sailed to the far-off Pacific Islands and saw fish that fly in the air.

"In the air!" Sally cried out, laughing. "Like sparrows? I don't believe it!"

"It's the bottom truth," Touch exclaimed.

41

But after a while, he found himself wishing he'd had better sense than to come to The Red Raven. What if he were a Jonah? He'd bring Sally to grief, harboring a runaway. If he had a horse, he'd be gone in the blink of an eye.

He asked suddenly, "How do you suppose The Great Chaffalo turned straw into horses?"

"He was a magician! They don't tell!"

"Where they real horses?"

She laughed lightly. "Real enough to bite."

"Did you ever see one?"

She nodded. "At a Fourth of July parade when I was little. A high-stepping horse came along at the end, all decked out in flags. There was no rider on its back. My pa said it was the work of The Great Chaffalo, keeping in practice."

"How could he know for certain?"

"It was a bay stallion, exactly like the one in the poster downstairs."

Touch leaned forward in great earnestness. "Where is The Great Chaffalo's summer house?"

"Just past the covered bridge," Sally replied. "There's a path leading off to the east. You're not thinking of going, Touch? Folks have seen wild dogs out that way."

42

"Got to. You haven't thrown that paper into the fire, the way Mr. Hobbs said. I can't stay here."

She rose and stood looking out the window, as if to avoid looking at the judge's document lying folded under a candlestick on the table. "No," she said at last. "I'm not going to throw it into the fire."

Touch waited a long time. And then he murmured, "Miss Sally, would you let me have a bundle of straw from the stable?"

# CHAPTER
# 7
# *Man in the Window*

**T**HE COVERED bridge gave off wisps of steam under the warming sun. Touch spared it only a glance and quickly followed a narrow, grassy path into the deep woods.

Carrying a bundle of fresh straw across his shoulder, he kept his eyes alert for wild dogs.

Finally, he caught sight of a large house with a shingled roof as full of holes as a moth-eaten shirt. A rocking chair, heavy with dust, still sat on the porch. Weeds shot up between the floorboards, and vines

44

were growing up through the chimney tops. The Great Chaffalo's place, Touch reckoned, and he threw the straw in a heap to the ground.

"Sir!" he called out. "The Great Chaffalo! My name's Touch, and I brought a bundle of straw. I'd be much obliged if you'd turn it into a horse."

Nearby, the tall weeds rasped a little in the breeze. But that was all.

He picked up the straw and hurried past broken windows to the rear of the house.

"You there, Mr. Chaffalo? It's me, Touch, and I'm in a dreadful hurry. My great-uncle aims to cart me off to the orphan house, but that don't take my fancy. I ain't asking for a fine, high-stepping horse, sir. Just any four legs'll do, as long as one ain't lame. I'd be proper grateful, Mr. Great Chaffalo."

Undiscouraged, Touch moved his bundle of straw back to the front of the house to try again. And he noticed the rocking chair was pitching as if someone had just got up.

Touch's hair went stiff as needles. But he was determined not to be scared off. He caught his breath.

"If you were dozing, I don't mean to rile you up, sir. Maybe you heard of my great-uncle. Judge Wigglesforth? Crosscut saws don't come any meaner. I know I don't amount to much, for a boy, but I'm not shifty-eyed, the way he says. I hope you can see that, Great Chaffalo."

Suddenly, Touch thought he could feel a pair of eyes watching him. The eyes in the poster! he thought. His hopes took a leap.

"I aim to ride through the woods until I'm long out of reach, sir. He won't know where to look. I'll thank you everlastingly if you'll oblige me with a horse."

A snarl burst out of the tall weeds. It wasn't a horse. It was a scruffy wild dog, its teeth looking like rusty nails. And it was coming straight for Touch.

Touch began to shinny up a porch column, but he knew that hound was going to get its rusty teeth into his leg. Then he heard a snap of fingers and a voice in the air.

"Hey! Hey!"

The bundle of straw changed into a horse.

Touch hadn't time for a gasp of astonishment. He jumped onto the horse's back. The beast whirled about and kicked its hind legs. The wild dog dodged

out of the way. With a cowed yelp, it vanished back into the weeds and woodland.

Touch caught his breath. He peered through a broken window and saw a face. The face of The Great Chaffalo.

"You saved me, for certain," declared Touch, his heart still banging away. "I'm mighty grateful, sir. And thankful for the horse."

For the first time Touch looked down at the high-legged stallion under him. It was a bay with a golden mane and a hide as fine as China silk.

"More'n I reckoned for, sir!" Touch exclaimed. "A plow horse would have done me fine. This must be the prettiest horse this side of sunset."

"It is," agreed The Great Chaffalo with an air of pride. "Although I might have done a tad better with the tail. I'm somewhat out of practice."

Touch felt bedazzled. "I can't imagine how you do it, sir!"

"A bit of straw and a touch of midnight," remarked The Great Chaffalo with a lofty smile. "It was a secret passed on to me by a Hey Hey Man in the Black Forest. A fellow trickster."

And Touch said, "I was in the coach early this

morning when you jumped on the roof."

"I do like to kick up my heels, now and then. Did I frighten you?"

"No, sir. Not exactly. I was almighty curious, though. I'd never seen a haunt before."

"A haunt! I've never haunted anything. I regard that as a slander. Do I look like a frail wisp of smoke?"

"No, sir," replied Touch quickly. "You look big as life."

"Bigger!" declared The Great Chaffalo, with a sharp lift of one eyebrow.

"Of course, sir," said Touch, becoming a little nervous.

The magician kept piercing him with his black poster eyes. "You must swear not to tell anyone how you came by this horse," said The Great Chaffalo. "I don't want every farm boy turning up with a bundle of straw."

"I swear it, sir."

"Ride on, Touch."

And with a snap of his long fingers, The Great Chaffalo was gone.

Touch lingered for a moment. Then he kicked the

horse's flanks lightly with his heels and started forward. He couldn't shake the feeling that eyes were still peering at him.

He turned for a backward glance. And he saw a face duck out of sight behind the trees. His eyes caught the flying tail of a dirt brown muffler.

Otis Cratt. Touch shrugged and continued on his way.

# CHAPTER
# 8

# *The Sheriff*

TOUCH AVOIDED the river road and kept to the woods on his way back to the village. He felt a blazing pride in owning the powerful, high-stepping stallion. He'd never before owned anything but his own shadow. He wished he could show the horse to Sally and Mr. Hobbs, but he couldn't go back on his word to The Great Chaffalo. He'd just take a moment to say good-bye, and be gone.

He hid the horse as best he could under the thick shelter of a chestnut tree. Be careful, he warned himself, not to let your great-uncle catch a peep of the horse. The judge would think you stole it and throw down thunderbolts of law.

If Sally was somewhere about The Red Raven Inn, Touch couldn't find her. He scratched out a short note, promising never to forget her, and left it under the candlestick in the upstairs parlor. He was sorry to see that the bill of sale was still there.

He followed the street, past the general store and the one-room bank, to the blacksmith's barn. With a bellows, Mr. Hobbs was pumping great gusts of air into the furnace.

"I've decided to run while I can," Touch said.

"On foot? You won't get far."

"Don't worry about me, sir. I've been in tighter squeaks than this before."

The blacksmith held out a hand, and Touch shook it. "You know your own mind. We'll miss having you around, Sally and me."

Touch hesitated, knowing that he was about to betray a confidence. "Sally doesn't aim to throw those papers into the fire, sir. They're still sitting upstairs under the candlestick. For certain, she's going to sell The Red Raven to my great-uncle."

The blacksmith heaved a weary sigh. "Sally knows her own mind, too. Good luck to you, Touch."

With his hands in his pockets, Touch ambled along the street as if he had nothing better to do. He crossed in front of a man on a gray horse riding into the village. The man's slouch hat was still wet from the night's rain. He had the gaze of a hawk and a sheriff's badge pinned to his coat. He gave Touch a friendly nod and tied up at the general store. Touch continued on his way.

Once into the trees, Touch lifted his feet and made for the stallion.

When he reached the chestnut tree, his heart caved in.

Where the horse had been now lay a pile of straw.

# CHAPTER
## 9
# *Followed*

**T**OUCH FELT betrayed. A watch began to chime, and his eyes flashed up into the tree. In long leather boots, The Great Chaffalo was standing on a limb with a walking stick tucked under his arm.

"That was mean and tricksy!" Touch exclaimed.

"Of course it was," said The Great Chaffalo. "I favor a bit of mischief now and then."

"I kept my word! I didn't tell a soul about you. And you turned the horse back into straw!"

The Great Chaffalo looked down, straight as a

plumb line. "That dirty, foul-smelling straw? You slander me again!"

For the first time, Touch noticed that the straw was moldy and sour. It wasn't the same pile of straw he'd brought from the inn!

"Did someone steal the horse and leave that smelly straw in its place?"

"Someone quite mean and tricksy."

"Otis Cratt!"

"Is that the fellow's name?" murmured The Great Chaffalo.

"He followed me!"

"Like a dog's tail."

"I was certain it was him I saw hiding near your summer house," Touch exclaimed.

"And not for the first time. The man's moved in again, quite uninvited. I must do something about him."

"Why did you let him make off with my horse?" Touch asked, bristling.

"It needed shoeing. I doubt that you have money to spare for that." From high up in the tree, The Great Chaffalo chuckled softly. "I can see him now, coming out of the blacksmith's barn. Well, look there! Something's put a fright into him. He's turned white as starch. He's racing the stallion this way. Wait on that stump over there. He was bound to come back looking for a boy clever as you."

"Clever?" Touch asked, suddenly mystified.

But before The Great Chaffalo would answer, he made himself disappear.

# CHAPTER
## 10

# *Otis Cratt*

 $I$N HIS tattered overcoat, with pockets deep as graves, Otis Cratt came flying back to the woods. He threw a quick look behind him and hauled up at the chestnut tree.

Touch glowered at him.

The pickpocket's face was still mummy-wrapped with the brown muffler. It was as if he couldn't abide the slightest chill in the air, Touch thought. Or was he fleeing from the law?

All night in the coach, he had kept peeping behind him. Now it dawned on Touch what had given Otis Cratt such a perishing fright in the village. He must have caught sight of the man in the rain-soaked hat: the sheriff, clinging to his heels like mud.

The pickpocket's knothole eyes cracked a smile. "How do, boy?"

"You stole my horse!"

"Of course I did," replied Otis Cratt in a rough, muffled voice. "You can make another anytime it suits you."

"What are you talking about?"

"I spied you make this one."

"Me? No, sir, you didn't," Touch exclaimed.

"Clever as they come, you are! That pile of straw jumped up into this fine beast. I watched you do it with me own eyes, and you just a shirttail boy!"

Touch felt a thunderclap of surprise. Hadn't Otis Cratt seen The Great Chaffalo through the broken window? Fire and furies! He believed Touch himself had the magic!

"You're not only a common horse thief," Touch declared, "you're addled. I can't do any such thing, and I'll be obliged if you'll get down off my horse."

Otis Cratt gave out a creaking little laugh. "I know

59

you ain't about to confess you're one of them witch and wizard folks. That's in the rule book, ain't it? But you can conjure anything you want."

"No, I can't."

Otis Cratt leaned forward and whispered, "Conjure me to be invisible."

"What?"

"Make me clear as window glass!"

Touch glanced upward into the trees, but The Great Chaffalo had left him to fend for himself.

"You might as well climb down off my horse," he said. "I ain't about to conjure anything."

"As soon as I'm turned invisible, I won't need a horse. You can have it back."

Touch took a long breath. He could calculate what was in the man's mind. Invisible, Otis Cratt could slip past the sheriff, bold as brass.

"Is it a bargain?" asked Otis Cratt.

And Touch glimpsed a way to get the man off his stallion. "If you promise not to tell a soul the secret of it."

"I never broke a promise yet," Otis Cratt murmured.

Touch knew a bald-faced lie when he heard it. He

cleared his throat and spoke with solemn dignity. "You'll need an oak leaf stuck in your hat," he said. "The topmost leaf. There's witchcraft in it, sir. Climb that tree over there and pick the topmost leaf. It'll turn you clear as window glass."

Otis Cratt gave out a soft chuckle, like a cat purring. "I wasn't born to be tricked by a shirttail boy. Soon as I'm up in that tree, you'll ride off. I'll wait here while you fetch that topmost leaf."

Touch tried to conceal his disappointment behind a smile. "I'll confess the thought crossed my mind. Wait here."

There was nothing for Touch to do but climb the tree and hope The Great Chaffalo would turn up, face-to-face. But the magician was leaving him to his own wits.

"You see anyone from up there?" called Otis Cratt.

Touch could see his great-uncle huffing and puffing to Sally in the middle of the road. "You looking for someone in particular, sir?"

"You see a man in a wet floppy hat?"

"Sure do. And there's Judge Wigglesforth. He goes hard on horse thieves."

"Hurry up with that oak leaf!"

When Touch returned to the ground, he carried himself with a bold air. If Otis Cratt was bound to be a gone-minded fool, Touch felt bound to help him. "Here it is, sir."

Otis Cratt stuck the oak leaf in his hatband.

"Hey! Hey!" said Touch.

And the horse thief asked, "Am I turned invisible?"

"I'll be skinned if you ain't."

"But I can still see me arms and legs."

"Of course you can," replied Touch. "But no one else can. Not another soul!"

Just then Touch heard a snap of fingers. A moment later, a dove came flying smack into Otis Cratt's chest.

"See that," declared Touch. "Not even birds can spy you. You're clear as window glass."

Suddenly, Otis Cratt fumbled in his deep coat pocket and hauled up a small leather pouch. He pulled open the drawstring and poured into his hand the three or four bright beads Touch had seen before.

"Did you turn these invisible, too?"

Touch pretended not to see anything. "What, sir?"

"These Pacific Island pearls! Can't you see 'em!"

A gasp of surprise caught in Touch's throat. His pa had once sailed to the Pacific Islands! And the pearls had come from his great-uncle's house. Did they rightfully belong to Touch?

At last, he said, "No, sir. I can't no more see 'em than the air itself. Not valuable, I hope."

"You fool! Pearl's are more'n worth their weight in gold! How am I going to sell 'em, if they're invisible?"

"Could be almighty difficult," said Touch. "Pacific Island pearls way out here! Imagine that."

"Turn 'em back so they shine again!" growled Otis Cratt.

"That's beyond me, sir." Touch began to offer up the best string of nonsense he could find in his head. "Stones stay magicked. They don't conjure like horses and grown men. By tomorrow you'll be good as new. But I reckon the pearls ain't worth dirt anymore."

Otis Cratt paused and then broke into a laugh. He flung the pearls to the leaves. "A trifling few.

There's a whole lot more where they came from, and I aim to get them. Must be a sackful! Each one shining like the morning star. And don't you conjure out their lights."

"No, sir," Touch muttered. There was no doubt in his mind that this was a treasure his pa had left to the judge's safekeeping. It was a sack of pearls his great-uncle had tried to befuddle Touch into signing away!

"I'll take that stallion," said Touch. "You gave your word."

Otis Cratt snickered. He pulled the muffler down around his neck as if he could breathe at last, now that he was invisible. "There's a pile of straw. Make yourself another horse."

For the first time, Touch saw the whole amazing show of Otis Cratt's face.

All of his teeth were gold.

# CHAPTER
# 11

# *The Burned Paper*

Touch was too dumbfounded to move.

Giving the horse a kick, Otis Cratt headed toward the village.

It's him! Touch thought. The man with gold teeth! The man who'd disappeared like a wisp of smoke from The Red Raven Inn. He hadn't been murdered! He was alive and kicking and loping off to the judge's place.

Touch, when he found his legs, let the pearls lie in

the leaves. They'd keep. He blue-streaked it for the village.

It seemed an eternity before The Red Raven came into view. Sally was no longer standing in the street, with his great-uncle huffing and puffing away at her. But his buggy was there, tied up to the hitch rail.

"Sally!" Touch shouted his lungs out and hoped he wasn't too late.

He banged through the door of the inn and met the glowering gaze of Judge Wigglesforth.

"Get out!" snapped the judge. "I've business to tidy up!"

At that moment, Sally came floating down the stairs with a folded document extended in her hand.

"The Red Raven is yours, Judge," she murmured. "You'll find the bill of sale has my signature, as you directed."

"Sally, hold back!" Touch cried out. "The man wasn't murdered! He's alive!"

"Poppycock!" exploded the judge, reaching out for the document.

Touch snatched the paper out of Sally's hand and flew out the door.

"Stop, thief!" bellowed Judge Wigglesforth.

His heart thumping madly, Touch raced to the blacksmith's barn. Mr. Hobbs turned from a dappled horse he was hitching to a spring wagon.

"Touch! You look like doom itself is chasing you!"

Judge Wigglesforth burst into the barn, with Sally close behind.

Touch reached the forge and threw the document into the fire. Flames rose like claws to grasp the paper and blacken it into ash.

"You meddling little thief!" the judge yelled. "Stealing right out of my hand! I've sent men to the gallows for less!"

"It was in my hand," Sally corrected him, and gave Touch a reassuring glance.

The judge snorted, and quickly recovered his cunning. "I'll write you out another bill of sale."

"Won't do you any good," Touch declared boldly. "There was no murder at The Red Raven. The man who disappeared is back."

"Stop talking rubbish," warned the judge.

"His name is Otis Cratt!"

The blacksmith's eyebrows jumped up. "That feller with his nose buried in a muffler?"

"Covering his teeth! And it was my great-uncle who sent for him again."

"What nature of slander is this?" the judge said, his face puffing up with anger.

Just then there came a familiar voice, shouting in the street.

"Otis Cratt!" said Touch. "See him for yourself!"

# The Invisible Man

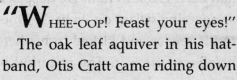

"WHEE-OOP! Feast your eyes!" The oak leaf aquiver in his hatband, Otis Cratt came riding down the street like a general on parade.

"Morning, ma'am!" he called out, lifting his hat politely to a woman along the walk. "Ain't you never seen a living ghost ride a horse?"

Touch saw that his overcoat pockets were bulging with plunder now. Otis Cratt must have gone through the judge's rooms, snatching up the treasure of pearls and whatever caught his eye.

Bold as thunder, Otis Cratt continued on down the street. "You, sir. What you gaping at, you flea-bit farmer? Stand and deliver! Throw up your cash money, if you got any!"

His mouthful of gold teeth were glinting in the sun. The judge gave out a quick, awful groan and went for his buggy. Sally appeared dazed with surprise. "It's him, Mr. Hobbs! It's him!"

"And someone must have let the air out of his head!" said the blacksmith.

Touch began to run. The high-stepping stallion had been given to him! He despised the sight of that swaggering villain on its back. Once Otis Cratt came to his senses and kicked in his heels, no one would be able to catch it. The beautiful bay would be lost forever.

"Where are you, Sheriff?" said Otis Cratt with a blustering laugh. "I've got you beat! You can't catch what you can't see. I'm turned invisible! Conjured clear as window glass!"

In his black buggy, Judge Wigglesforth was bearing down like a windstorm.

"You in the bank!" shouted Otis Cratt, stepping down from the stallion. "I've got deep pockets! You won't mind if I help myself."

The judge was waving his buggy whip as if it were a club. "You crackbrained oaf! Get out of here!"

Otis Cratt turned. "Howdy, Judge. But I got no need to do your bidding anymore. No, sir!"

The whip whistled down, and Otis Cratt jumped behind the stallion for shelter.

"Back off, Judge!"

"Mangy scum!" said the judge. "Cover your face! Go away! You're no more invisible than a tree!"

"I been conjured!"

"You've been hoodwinked!"

The bellowings had drawn villagers into the street. The first mutterings were now breaking into shouts.

"The man with gold teeth!"

"It's him! The disappeared man!"

"His bones don't lie under The Red Raven!"

"Look at them teeth! He wasn't murdered!"

Touch reached the stallion and leaped onto its

back from the clear side. Dodging the buggy whip, Otis Cratt mounted from the left at the same moment.

"Boy!" Otis Cratt exploded. "You befooled me! I'll twist your neck!"

But with the whip popping around him like fireworks, Otis Cratt dug his heels into the horse.

The stallion bolted, and Touch grabbed his arms around its neck. When he looked back, he saw men running and pitching stones.

The judge followed in his buggy, as if trying to whip Otis Cratt into eternity. Not far behind came Mr. Hobbs on the spring wagon, with Sally on the seat beside him.

The horse flew along the river road. Touch clung like paint. He hoped a low tree branch might sweep Otis Cratt to the ground. He could hear a jingling from Otis Cratt's pockets, as if the judge's silver knives and forks were stuffed among the pearls.

The stallion was leaving the black buggy far behind. The covered bridge loomed up ahead.

Touch felt Otis Cratt's long-fingered hand close

around his neck. "Clear as window glass, was I? I aim to wring your scrawny neck one-handed!"

"You befooled yourself!" Touch said. "I only wanted my horse back!"

Suddenly, the hand vanished from his neck. Otis Cratt grabbed great fistfuls of the horse's mane and hauled back. Touch caught a gulp of air.

Up ahead, on the narrow path from The Great Chaffalo's summer house, appeared the sheriff in his floppy hat.

"Gold Teeth!" he yelled, and prodded his horse to a gallop.

Otis Cratt swung the stallion around, back along the road. And there ahead charged Judge Wigglesforth, his buggy whip still streaking the air, and Mr. Hobbs close behind.

Otis Cratt turned off into the trees toward the white-rushing river. Touch felt a powerful jerk on the back of his neck and then found himself flung to the ground like extra baggage.

Touch picked himself up and stood for an instant. He could see at once what was going to happen. Otis Cratt had lightened the load on the horse. He

was going to try to leap the banks of the river on the fine, high-stepping stallion.

"You'll break his legs!" Touch called out desperately.

Touch rushed forward. He caught a glimpse far-off of his great-uncle heading the buggy into the trees and overturning. He kept running. He needed a last look at the horse that had once been his, that horse prettier than a sunset.

He stumbled over the tattered overcoat. Otis Cratt had shucked it, with its heavy pockets.

"No horse can make a jump like that!" he yelled, blinking back tears.

He heard the stallion give out a whinny. Touch dodged past another tree and caught sight of Otis Cratt leaping the high banks of the river.

"Hey! Hey!"

In midair, the bay stallion turned to wisps of straw in the wind.

Otis Cratt tumbled, all arms and legs, into the river.

Touch wiped his nose in the sudden flush of a smile. He should have known better than to torment himself about the stallion. He gazed upward into the tree and saw The Great Chaffalo. The magician smiled with his black poster eyes and tipped his hat. And then he was gone, to the chiming of a watch.

# CHAPTER
## 13

## *Black Magic*

**THE SHERIFF** rode down into the river and hauled Otis Cratt out of the water like a flapping trout.

Touch caught sight of far-off villagers watching along the bank. And his great-uncle was back on his feet, pointing his whip and advising the sheriff to let the rascal drown, legal and proper. He'd been too late to see the horse turn to straw.

Everyone would know the work of The Great Chaffalo, Touch thought.

But Touch was wrong.

■ ■ ■

For days Otis Cratt's overcoat, with its pockets heavy enough to ballast a ship, hung on the rack in The Red Raven Inn. It had been lightened only by a leather pouch the size of a fist.

Among the Pacific Island pearls was a letter to Touch from his pa, to be read when he was grown-up. Touch had felt grown-up enough to read it. The letter embraced him like strong arms, and he'd shed a few tears. He valued the words more than the pearls. The blacksmith had walked with Touch to the bank to place the pouch in safekeeping.

More than once Mr. Hobbs had gone banging on the judge's door. "The greedy muckworm has locked himself in," he reported. "People are talking. Tongues are busy!"

Before the fire in the public room, the blacksmith unraveled the judge's scheme. To lay hands on the thriving inn, he'd put Otis Cratt up to signing the register and flashing his gold teeth all around the village. When the inn was dead asleep, Otis Cratt had slipped out, leaving a barber's case behind.

Touch knew he'd hidden himself in the summer house at first. The Great Chaffalo had seen him there. A night or two later, Otis Cratt must have slipped out of the valley.

"Then the judge started rumoring that the barber had been murdered for his gold teeth," said Mr. Hobbs with a scowl. "Crime and motive, as he put it! Buying miserly cheap was what he had in mind! When the travelers got wind of murder and buried bones, they stopped putting up here."

"And I came within seconds of handing the inn over to him on a fiddling piece of paper," Sally exclaimed angrily.

Mr. Hobbs nodded. "Touch was good luck on two legs—there in the very nick of time."

Touch felt a smile deep inside himself as Sally reached out a hand to him. He wasn't a Jonah. No, by dogs, he wasn't!

The blacksmith poked up the fire as if it were the judge's own guts in there. "The judge sent for Otis Cratt again. He calculated The Red Raven would be resting in the palm of his hand by time the coach arrived this morning. And then, behold! The man with gold teeth would turn up alive, after all! The plague of murder would be lifted, and the inn would thrive again."

81

Sally's eyes were aflame. "My father went to his grave!"

"But now the judge seems to have dug a grave for himself," said the blacksmith, with clear satisfaction. "Tongues are wagging!"

"Saying what, Mr. Hobbs?"

"The old witchcraft! A horse disappearing in mid-air!"

Touch gazed at Mr. Hobbs. Hadn't anyone seen the straw floating away with the breeze? Had everyone but Touch been too far-off to notice?

"Folks always said the judge must know the devil by his first name. Now they believe it!" Mr. Hobbs remarked. "They saw him along the river waving a black stick."

"It was his buggy whip," said Touch.

"A conjuring stick. And yelling dark bejabbers to turn the horse into the air itself. Black magic!"

Touch stood in amazement. No one had recognized the wonder hand of The Great Chaffalo!

Mr. Hobbs poked the fire again. "Folks are throwing stones at the judge's house. He'll waste away behind his locked doors, afraid to show his face!"

．　．　．

In the days that followed, travelers again began stopping at The Red Raven Inn. And Touch made himself useful, glad to chop wood and meet the coach when it arrived. He didn't want to think about the treasure of pearls sitting in the bank. His pa had meant that for when he was full grown.

One damp afternoon, he returned to the chestnut tree where Otis Cratt had scattered the invisible pearls. They were easy to find among the leaves, each one bright as the morning star. Touch meant to give them to Sally, if she'd have them.

He found himself listening for the chiming of a watch. But the air remained still. He wondered how The Great Chaffalo had pinched a Chinese coin off the end of Mr. Hobbs's nose.

Before long he'd walk out to the summer house. Maybe The Great Chaffalo would teach him how to do it.